AF291488

THIS BOOK BELONGS TO:

First published in 2024 by HarperCollins *Children's Books*
An imprint of HarperCollins *Publishers* India
4th Floor, Tower A, Building No. 10, DLF Cyber City,
DLF Phase II, Gurugram, Haryana – 122002

www.harpercollins.co.in

2 4 6 8 10 9 7 5 3 1

P-ISBN: 978-93-6569-576-2
E-ISBN: 978-93-6569-042-2

Design, inside illustrations and cover: EMoMee Entertainment Private Limited

Printed and bound at
Nutech Print Services - India

HarperCollinsIn

I DID A BOO BOO

A BOOK ABOUT LEARNING FROM MISTAKES AND BOUNCING BACK!

On a Friday evening,
Little Mo sat on a stool,

When all the kids
were back home from school.

Mo's face was worried –
Cheeks were red
Eyes had tears,
And just then Mo said,

"I did a boo boo!
What should I do?
My mommy's bowl
is broken in two!

Ask the child: Can you think of a time you felt worried because you made a mistake? What was the mistake and why did that worry you?

She always says
the bowl looks so lovely,
It's always on the table
with fruit so yummy.

It had some berries
that were oh-so-blue,

Now they're on the floor
And I just ate two!!

It was too high
above the ground,
I reached up high
and it fell down.

Now it's in pieces –
on the floor,

Under the table
and near the door.

I feel bad,
I feel sad,

I'm also worried
That she'll be mad!!

Ask the child: What helps you when you feel sad?

Look what I've done
And now I don't know what to do,
I made a mess,
Do I stick it with glue?

Ask the child: What do you think Mo can do about this mistake?

Daddy always says
To be careful
To be sure,
When I help him
wash the dishes
Or clean up the floor.

I am bad,
I am sad,

I'm so worried that
mommy and daddy will be mad!!"

Ask the child: What would you do if you think mommy and daddy
will be angry with you about something?

And just then
as Mo started to cry,
Mommy and daddy
came inside to ask why.

"I'm sorry mommy
I did a boo boo,
I wanted berries
and the bowl broke in two.

I am bad
And now you are sad.
I'm so sorry,
Please don't be mad.

I was not careful
And it fell down
Now there are pieces
All over the ground."

Ask the child: What are the different ways in which you have not been careful before?

Mommy let out a sigh
and gave Mo a hug,
Daddy smiled
with a wink and a shrug.

"My little Mo
You broke the bowl,
Now, there are pieces
And berries on the floor.

You were not careful
And I feel sad,
But that does not mean
You are bad.

We all make boo boos
Yes, we all do,
But always remember
To learn from them too.

Ask the child: What all could Mo do the next time he wants berries from the bowl on the table?

Now while daddy
cleans the floor,
You clear the mess
of berries at the door."

Mommy kissed Mo
Daddy hugged Mo too.
Mo felt safe
And loved too.

A broom to sweep,
a cloth to wipe,
The mess was clean
with one swipe.

Mo felt safe
But still felt sad,
"I'll be careful next time
I stick out my hand.

We all make boo boos
Yes, even me and you.
But, if we learn from them
and don't repeat,
Then, one boo boo
does not become two."

Ask the child: What are some mistakes that you have learnt from and not repeated? I can begin by sharing an example of my own!

ABOUT EMOMEE

At EMoMee, we believe the journey to becoming an emotionally intelligent leader starts in early childhood. We're dedicated to weaving emotional intelligence into the fabric of everyday life for kids, parents, caregivers and educators. By turning daily activities into opportunities for emotional growth, we help develop habits that bring about meaningful changes in behaviour.

Join us on our mission to equip children with the skills they need to navigate life's complex challenges with grace, resilience and confidence.

ABOUT THE AUTHOR

Varun Duggirala is a seasoned entrepreneur and thought leader who co-founded EMoMee to enhance children's emotional intelligence through innovative educational content and products. With extensive expertise in marketing and storytelling, he creates resources on emotional intelligence that resonate with professionals, parents and educators.

As an author and popular podcaster, Varun delves into topics from entrepreneurship to parenting, making complex ideas accessible and relatable. He is a trusted voice in creative and entrepreneurial circles, while also consistently focusing on the practical joys and challenges of parenting.

MORE FROM EMOMEE

EMoMee's Shape Sorter Kit

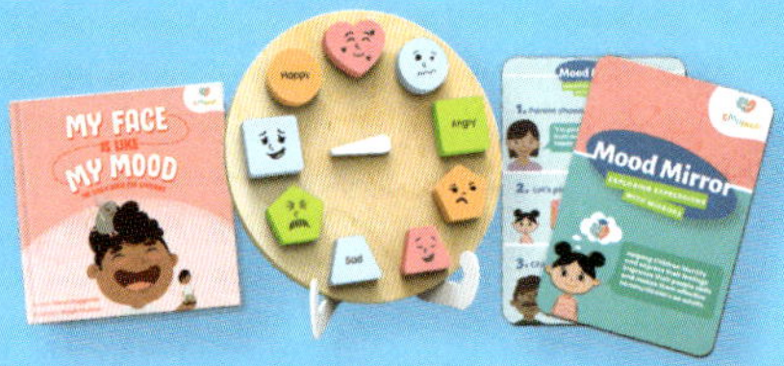

EMoMee's ABC Kit

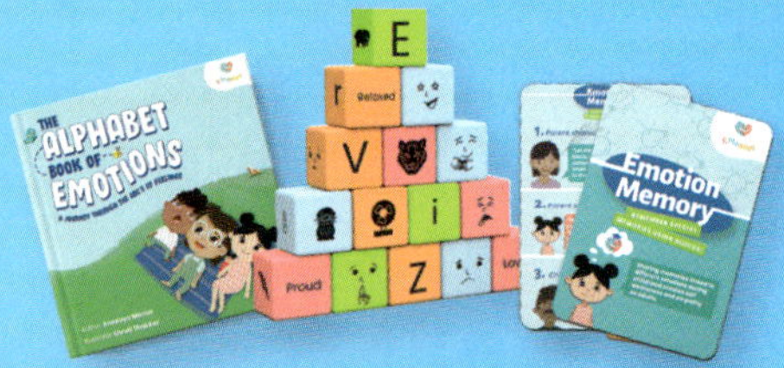

EMoMee's Playground Adventure Kit

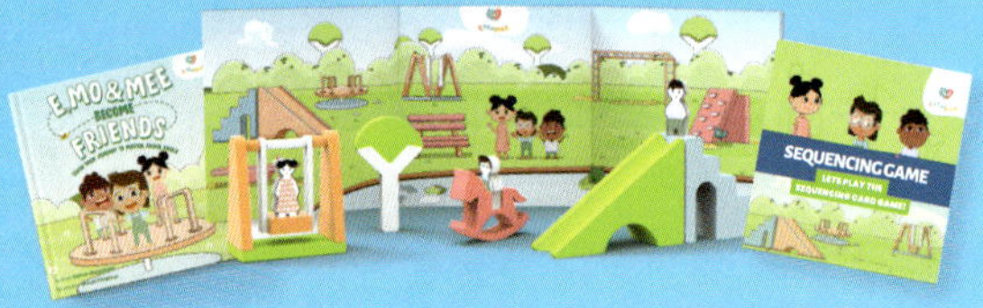

Other Books With HarperCollins

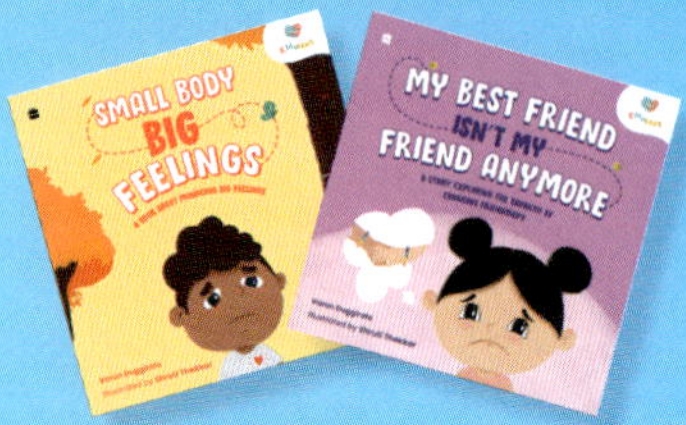

Use code **EQBUILDERS10** to get 10% off on our toys, games and books!

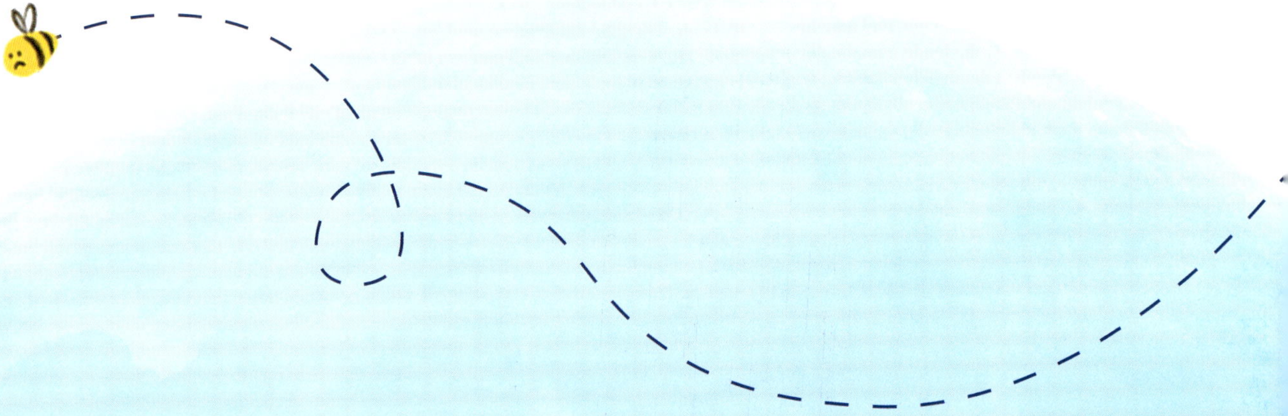